HARE and TORTOISE Race Across ISRAEL

For the educators of the Ohr Kodesh Early Childhood Center and the Temple Shalom Religious School in Chevy Chase, Maryland. Thank you for the rich, joyful Jewish education you provide.
—L. G.

To Fred
—S. G.

KAR-BEN PUBLISHING
An imprint of Lerner Publishing Group, Inc.
241 First Avenue North
Minneapolis, MN 55401 USA
1-800-4-KARBEN

Website address: www.karben.com

Main body text set in Futura Std Light Condensed.
Typeface provided by Adobe Systems.

Library of Congress Cataloging-in-Publication Data

Gehl, Laura.
Hare and Tortoise race across Israel / by Laura Gehl ; illustrated by Sarah Goodreau.
  pages   cm
Summary: Two good friends, Hare and Tortoise, race from Tel Aviv to the Dead Sea,
enjoying the unique culture and geography of Israel along the way.
ISBN 978–1–4677–2199–8 (lib. bdg. : alk. paper)
ISBN 978–1–4677–6202–1 (eBook)
[1. Fables. 2. Folklore.] I. Goodreau, Sarah, illustrator. II. Aesop. III. Title.
PZ8.2.G38Har 2015
398.2—dc23 [E]   2014003669

Manufactured in China
3-1008714-15938-8/4/2022

0423/B0604/A5

HARE and TORTOISE Race Across ISRAEL

LAURA GEHL
ILLUSTRATIONS BY SARAH GOODREAU

KAR-BEN PUBLISHING

HARE and TORTOISE lived together near the Hashalom train station in Tel Aviv.

On sunny days,
they frolicked at the beach.

On rainy days, they visited museums.

At night, the two friends dined on carrots and hummus before attending the opera.

One morning, Hare and Tortoise watched the trains come and go. "I **think** I'm **as fast as those trains**," Hare said. "**Maybe faster.**"

Tortoise giggled. "You are fast, my friend, but you are not as fast as a train."

Hare did not laugh. "Well, I may not be as fast as a train, but I am certainly faster than *you*," he said.

Tortoise ignored Hare's bragging and held out a bag. "Would you like some rugelach?" he offered. "I just stopped by the bakery."

But Hare refused to be distracted. "I *am* faster than you," he repeated. "I could beat you in any race, anytime, anywhere."

"What about in a race all the way to the Dead Sea?" Tortoise asked. "Do you think you could beat me?"

"Of course!" Hare said.

"We'll see," Tortoise replied.
"Remember the sign that says
'Welcome to the Dead Sea?'
That will be our finish line."

THE NEXT DAY, the two friends began their race. They left the busy traffic of Tel Aviv and continued into the countryside.

Hare hopped through olive groves and past persimmon trees. Behind him, he heard Tortoise calling "**shalom**" to everyone he passed. Hare did not waste time chatting with other animals. He leaped further and further ahead.

When Hare reached Jerusalem, he stopped at the shuk to
buy dried apricots. "**I am so far ahead**," he thought.
"**I can take a short break.**"

Hare watched a ball game in Independence Park.

Then he sat on the sidewalk near a group of street performers. As he listened to the music and admired the dancers, Hare completely forgot about the race. Suddenly he felt somobody tap his shoulder. It was Tortoise.

"Want to share my falafel?" his friend asked.

Hare couldn't believe Tortoise had caught up. Quickly he bounded away, not even taking time to say "No thank you."

DEAD SEA

Hare left Jerusalem in a hurry and hopped his way through the Judean Hills into the desert. He didn't stop until he reached an oasis.

Hare sat in a tent, enjoying a cup of tea and flaky baklava. "I wish I could ride a camel the rest of the way to the Dead Sea," Hare admitted to his Bedouin host.

ברוכים הבאים
לים המלח
WELCOME TO THE
DEAD SEA

When Hare at last saw the
sea ahead, he was so exhausted
he could not hop the final stretch
to the finish line. **"I'll just
sit for a moment,"** he
thought, collapsing by a palm
tree. But the bright sun made
Hare want to close his eyes.

Hare awoke to the song of a raven. He jumped, looking back to see if Tortoise might be close to catching up. But he couldn't see Tortoise anywhere behind him. Then Hare looked ahead toward the sea. "OH NO!" he exclaimed.

ברוכים הבאים
לים המלח
WELCOME TO THE
DEAD SEA

Off in the distance, he saw Tortoise slowly but surely approaching the finish line. Hare took off as fast as he could. He leaped and bounded and bounded and leaped. But Tortoise reached the sign just ahead of Hare.

"I lost the race," Hare said, sadly. "I guess I was too sure of myself. And now I'm all hot and sweaty, and my muscles ache."

"Slow and steady might win the race, but I'm hot and sore, too," Tortoise said. He pointed toward the Dead Sea, where many other animals floated happily in the salty water just a few yards away. "Race you into the water," Tortoise giggled.

ירושלים
JERUSALEM

DEAD SEA

DEAD SEA

LAURA GEHL

Laura Gehl's previous books include *And Then Another Sheep Turned Up* (Kar-Ben Publishing) and *One Big Pair of Underwear* (Beach Lane Books). She lives with her husband and four children in Chevy Chase, Maryland... approximately 6,000 miles from Tel Aviv.

SARAH GOODREAU

Sarah Goodreau was born and raised in Massachusetts. She studied at the Savannah College of Art and Design. Besides illustrating she loves working on short stop-motion animations and exploring the city with her little dog, Potemkin. She lives in Amsterdam, The Netherlands.